Milton the Early Riser

BY ROBERT KRAUS
PICTURES BY JOSE ARUEGO AND ARIANE DEWEY

Aladdin Paperbacks
New York   London   Toronto   Sydney

ALADDIN PAPERBACKS

An imprint of Simon & Schuster Children's Publishing Division

1230 Avenue of the Americas, New York, NY 10020

Text copyright © 1972 by Robert Kraus

Illustrations copyright © 1972 by Jose Aruego

ALADDIN PAPERBACKS, Stories to Go!, and colophon are trademarks of Simon & Schuster, Inc.

Manufactured in the United States of America

First Aladdin Paperbacks edition April 1987

First Aladdin Stories to Go! edition June 2006

2 4 6 8 10 9 7 5 3 1

The Library of Congress has cataloged the hardcover edition as follows:

Kraus, Robert, 1925-

Milton the early riser / by Robert Kraus : pictures by Jose Aruego & Ariane Dewey

p. cm

Summary: The first one to awaken, Milton the Panda tries hard to wake all the other animals, but to no avail.

[1. Pandas—Fiction.] I. Aruego, Jose, ill. II. Dewey, Ariane, ill. III. Title.

PZ7K868Mb 1987

[E]—dc19 87-32072 CIP AC

ISBN 0-671-66272-4 (hc.)

ISBN-13: 978-0-671-66911-9 (Aladdin pbk.)

ISBN-10: 0-671-66911-7 (Aladdin pbk.)

ISBN-13: 978-1-4169-1856-1 (Stories to Go! pbk.)

ISBN-10: 1-4169-1856-6 (Stories to Go! pbk.)

For
Pamela, Bruce, Billy,
and Juan

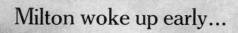

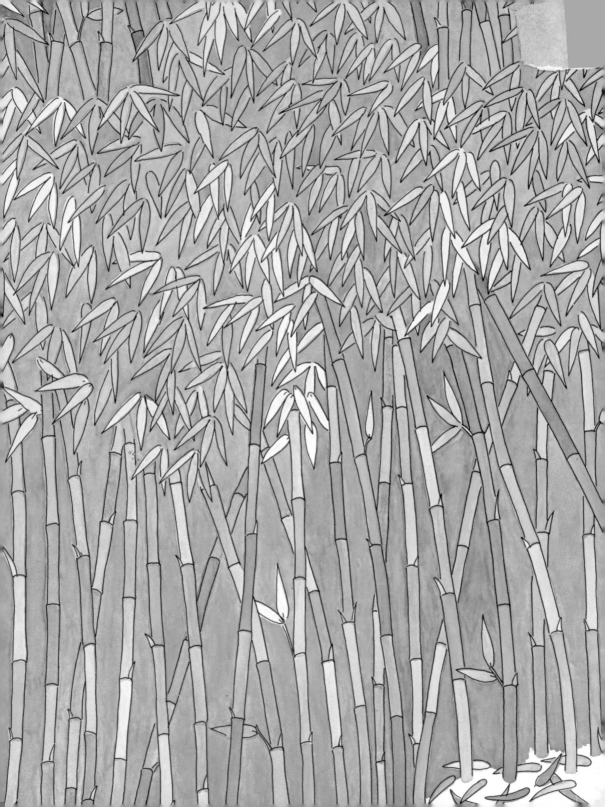

and went out to play.
But there was nobody to play with.

The Creeps next door were still asleep.

So were the Whippersnappers across the way

and the Nincompoops in the back.

The whole world seemed to be asleep.

So Milton watched television.

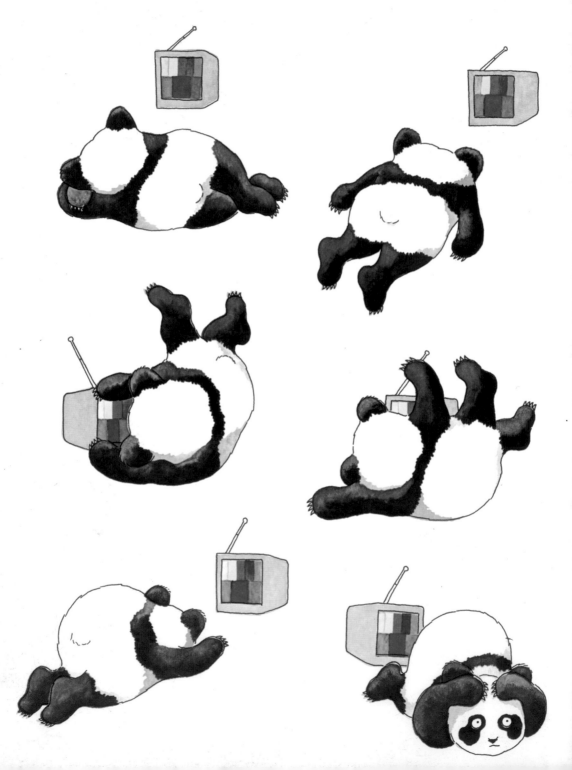

And the sleepers slept on.

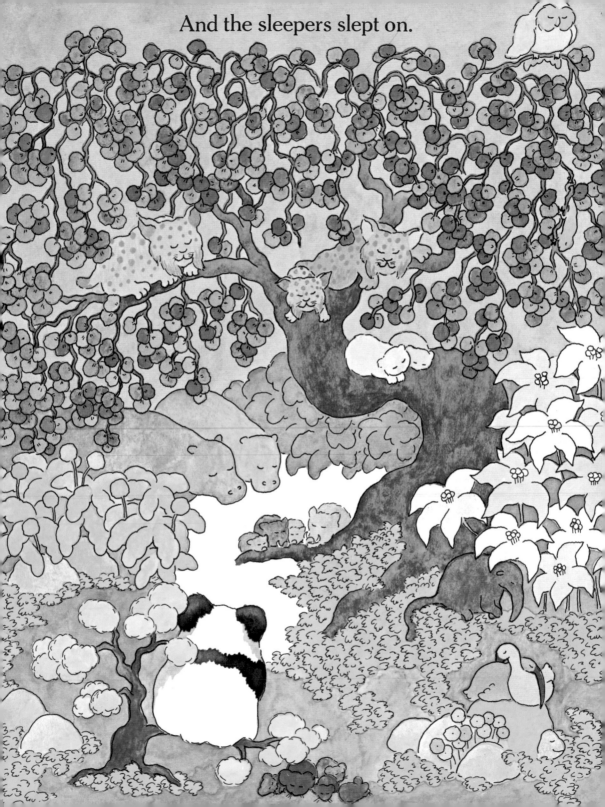

Milton jumped up and down.

But the sleepers slept on.

Milton danced and did tricks.

Yet the sleepers slept on.

Then Milton sang up a storm.

The mountains shook.
The trees trembled.

And a whirlwind blew the sleepers out of bed!

Still the sleepers slept on.

"Oh dear," said Milton. "What a mess."

And he worked and worked
and he put things right.

Just as everybody woke up.

Everybody but Milton.

"Rise and shine," said Milton's father.
"Wake up sleepy-head," said Milton's mother.
Milton the early riser didn't hear a word.

He was fast asleep.